T0368520

THE THREE BEST FRIENDS AND THE HOT AIR BALLOON FESTIVAL

BOOK 3   BY DEACON GABE GAGNÉ

THE THREE BEST FRIENDS

AND

THE HOT AIR

BALLOON

FESTIVAL

ACKOWLEDGEMENTS:
Thanks to:
Cecile Paquette
    for her suggestions
    and corrections
Anna Gagne
    for her encouragements
    and suggestions

WRITTEN & ILLUSTRATED

by DEACON GABE GAGNÉ

BOOK 3

The adventures of Three Best Friends
book 3
The Adventure at the Hot Air Balloon Festival

Life on the Island was about to pick up speed. As soon as the tourists arrived the lives of our trio of best friends would be very busy.

They all had found jobs tending the sales counters of the several businesses that catered to the needs of the vacationers.

But this Sunday the season was opening with a Hot Air Balloon festival.

Before that took place there would be a Sunday service at the church after which there would be a picnic.

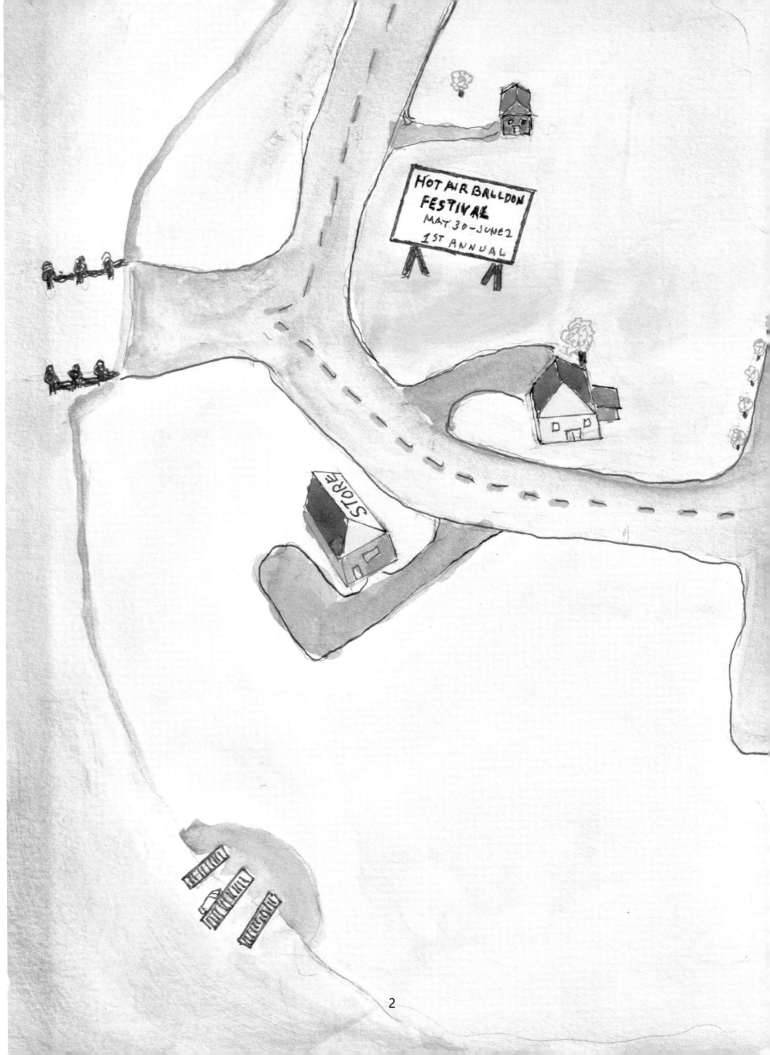

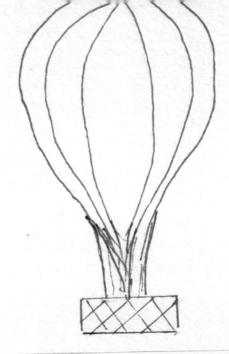

The congregation was surprised and glad to see that Suzie's Gramm had joined them. It was a beautiful service and a prayer was said to bless the summer's activities.

Our trio of friends were busy helping with setting up the picnic tables outdoors. They were eager to hear what Gramm had to report about the big City.

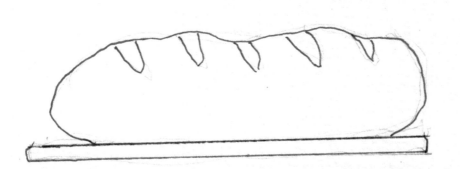

Finally, everyone was seated at the tables and after prayer before meals was said, the boisterous crowd grew quiet while they all enjoyed a delightful pot luck.

Finally, it was time for cake and ice cream. The desserts were already on the table, but first Gramm had something to say and it couldn't wait. So, everyone politely listened to their guest.

She told of the wonderful actions of the boys who retrieved her little dog and saved the day! She couldn't stop praising them. Someone started to applaud and the others joined in. And it was thus that finally the cake and ice cream got tasted and they were delicious!

From where they were, they could see the hot air balloons beginning to rise above the horizon.

This was the first time the island had hosted such an event. There was sure to be to a great time enjoyed by all.

Gramm had driven her car to the event with the intention of leaving it there for the trio to install the anti-theft device. So she had parked nearby. Suzie exclaimed to Gramm that it was a beautiful car and she loved the color!

As soon as the boys saw it, they were ecstatic and Johnny could not keep himself from inspecting it from one end to the other. He finally exclaimed: "This is the finest example of a classic car of its kind." He continued:" Gramm, tell me if I'm wrong, but isn't that a '57 Chevrolet BEL-AIR 2 door hard top with a 283 cubic inch displacement V8 engine with a power glide transmission?"

Gramm exclaimed: "You are right on all counts." And she told us further that her father had purchased it new many years ago.

She loved that car and every one could see why she didn't want it stolen.

The team of three said working on it would be their top priority.

8

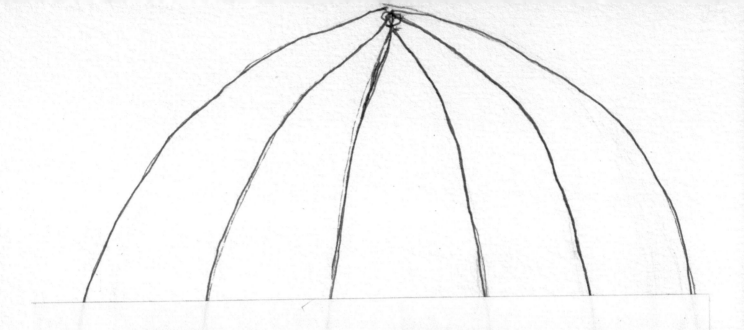

The balloons were now ready to offer rides to the public. Our trio quickly got in line to buy tickets. It wasn't long before it was their turn and there was no problem for Johnny's wheel chair.

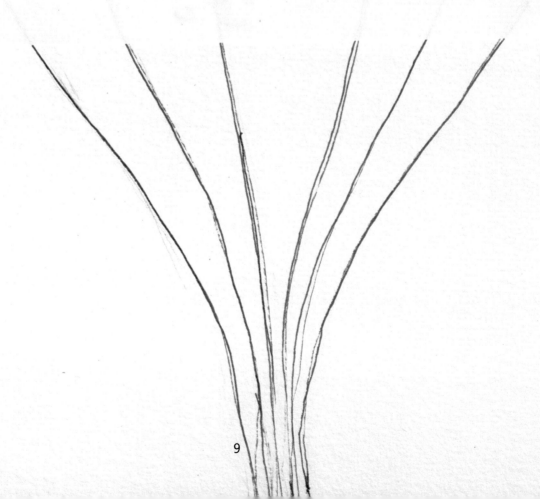

I THINK I'LL STAY
HERE WITH YOU !

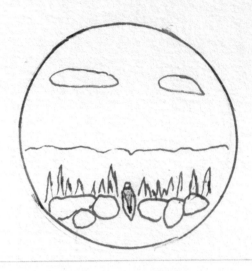

Up they went! And Suzie had remembered to bring her father's field glasses!

The view was fantastic. They could see the whole island. They could see even the far shore which was deserted because of the large boulders and jagged rock peaks which were strewn along the beach. That part of the island seemed as inhospitable as people said.

To Suzie's amazement, with the field glasses she saw a small boat that had been pulled up and seemingly hidden between the rocks. Nobody ever went there! So, it was strange to be sure! The boys took turns looking with the field glasses.
Each of the three had a theory about the boat.

Finally, the ride came to an end and they descended to the ground. The boys had noticed that the balloon basket was attached to a sturdy rope which was itself attached to a giant winch on the ground which was now being rewound.

The three were very excited. They described to Gramm, Billy's grandmother and the other family members the sights they saw from 400 feet up!

But amongst themselves they expressed their shared suspicions about the small boat they had seen among the boulders and jagged rocks!

Before long there was a commotion coming from where they had climbed aboard for their ride. Someone was yelling: "Help, stop that man he stole all the ride money! He is getting away with it! Someone please stop him!"

The thief had taken off running through the tall marsh grass heading towards the rocky side of the island!

At once the three best friends came together where Johnny was in his wheel chair. Suzie exclaims: "I bet he's trying to get to that boat!" The boys said in unison:" YUP!"
"We have to stop him", she exclaimed!
Johnny said: " But I can't catch up with him with my wheelchair! The grass is much too thick and high for it!"

Then Johnny had an idea and as they huddled together, Johnny's proposal seemed possible. Yes, they could do it!

HELP!
STOP THAT
THIEF!

16

Suzie immediately goes to Gramm and whisperes in her ear the plan they had concocted and Gramm nodded her OK. Although she had some uneasiness, she kept it to herself knowing the trio could be trusted.

At once Suzie jumps into Gramm's car and gets behind the wheel! Billy gets into the seat next to her! Shortly the car starts towards the tall grass and the thief!

It doesn't take long for the Suzie to catch up to the perpetrator who seems to be having some trouble with the thick grass himself! Soon they're next to him and Billy shouts out through the open window : "You'd better give up fella you're not going to get to your getaway boat!"

Seeing he was not cooperating, Billy opens the long door and pushes it onto the crook. He immediately loses his balance and falls into the thick grass.

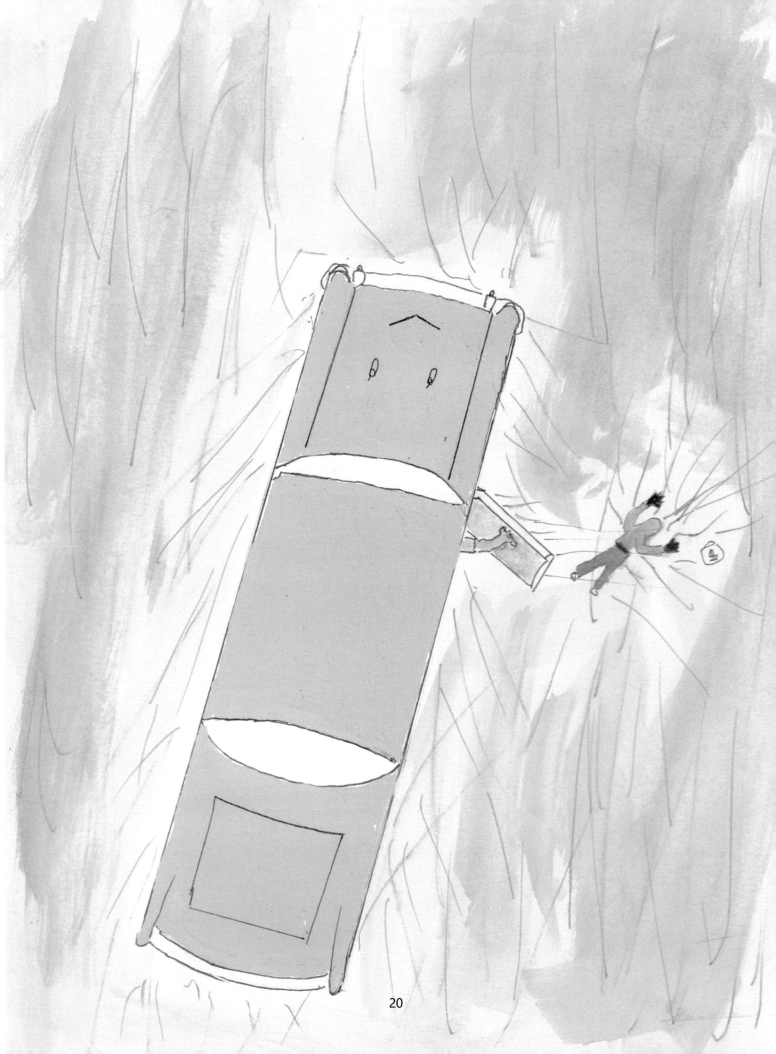

That's when Billy quickly jumps out of the car and runs over to the crook and grabs the money bag that he had dropped.

He quickly gets back into the car and Suzie turns the car around and they rejoin Johnny who's now smiling broadly!

Johnny's plan had worked perfectly.

Eventually the guard went up with the balloonist and radioed the police officer on the ground telling him the location of the thief!

The thief was caught! But the police officer came to Billy and said to him: "I'm glad you didn't tangle with this crook because he was armed and dangerous"! He also added that they had reliable info that this was the same crook that stole the little dog that day in the city.

"So that wraps that case" exclaimed Billy.

The police officer was so impressed with the trio that he put their names in for a commendation.

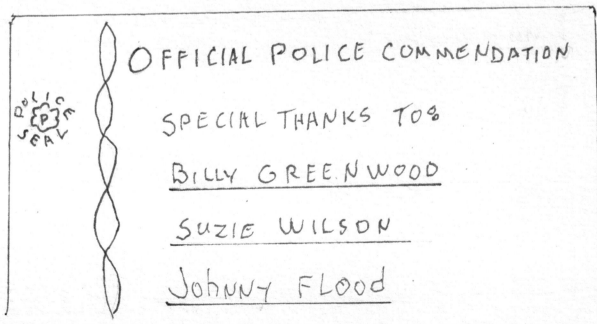

OFFICIAL POLICE COMMENDATION

SPECIAL THANKS TO:

BILLY GREENWOOD

SUZIE WILSON

Johnny Flood

POLICE SEAL

The balloonist's money was returned and after parking the '57 Chevy they all regrouped with Gramm and the others.

Gramm actually hadn't known that Suzie had taken driver's ed. Never the less, she triumphantly said: "I knew Suzie could do it." That was only partially true. Deep down though she was glad that she had not said anything about her doubts!

She continued eloquently (as only she could) and gave great credit to all three of the teenagers.
She finally finished by proclaiming the three a great team!

Then suddenly all the people at once started to applaud and Gramm's speech came to a close! And she took a small bow!
The three teenagers all said they were only too glad to help.

Our trio of best friends had worked as a team! They all had played a part in capturing the thief and their families were very justifiably proud of them!

The festival continued without any more interruptions. The day was a success!

All too soon, it was time for Gramm to return to the big city but they all prevailed on her to stay for a couple days longer while the team installed the anti-theft device. She very willingly accepted the hospitality.

After two days it was time for her to go. This time they all wished her a good trip. But before she left the trio gave her instructions.

They said: "Be sure to use your key to lock and unlock your car and make sure your security cameras are working." And after assuring them of that she was on her way!

After they all had waved good bye as Gramm drove away they reminisced about the events of the day.

And it was agreed by all that the team of three had saved the day. The team had triumphed again!

At this moment in time nothing seemed impossible for them! Nothing at all!

However, amongst themselves they wondered whether their anti-car theft system on Gramm's car would be successful??   It remained to be seen!

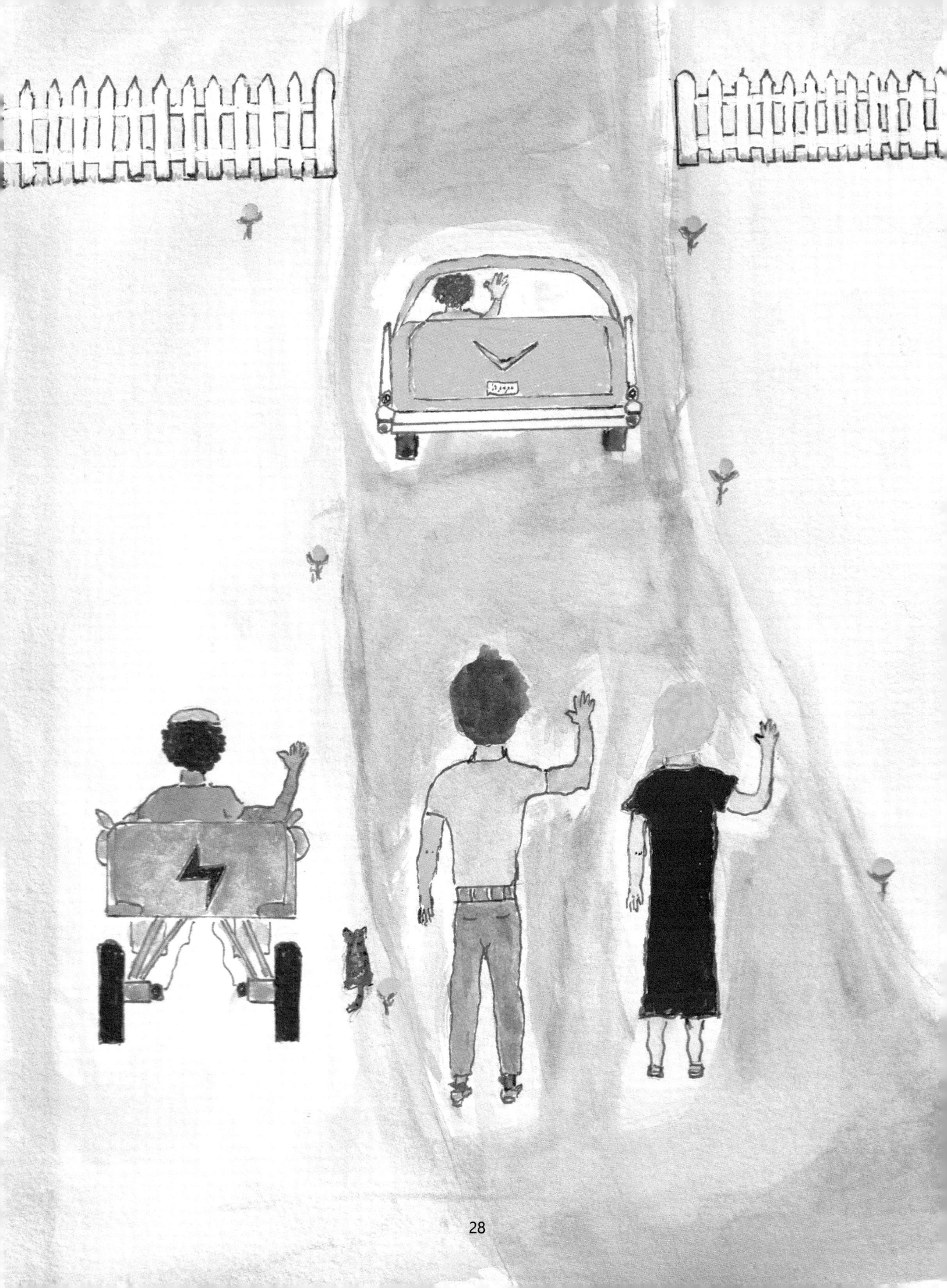

The END of THIS ADVENTURE

LOOK FOR

THE NEXT ONE

AuthorHouse™
1663 Liberty Drive
Bloomington, IN 47403
www.authorhouse.com
Phone: 833-262-8899

Because of the dynamic nature of the Internet, any web addresses or links contained in this book may have changed
since publication and may no longer be valid. The views expressed in this work are solely those of the author and do
not necessarily reflect the views of the publisher, and the publisher hereby disclaims any responsibility for them.

Any people depicted in stock imagery provided by Getty Images are models,
and such images are being used for illustrative purposes only.
Certain stock imagery © Getty Images.

This book is printed on acid-free paper.

ISBN: 979-8-8230-4025-9 (sc)
ISBN: 979-8-8230-4026-6 (e)

Library of Congress Control Number: 2024926822

Print information available on the last page.

Published by AuthorHouse 01/17/2025

authorHOUSE®

Printed in the United States
by Baker & Taylor Publisher Services